GW01402719

The Wonderland Show

The Vendetta Saga, Volume 4

Arianna Courson

Published by Arianna Courson, 2024.

THE WONDERLAND SHOW

First edition. November 3, 2024.

Copyright © 2024 Arianna Courson.

ISBN: 979-8227270634

Written by Arianna Courson.

Also by Arianna Courson

Table of Contents

to you, thank you for supporting my dream of being an author

Act IV – The Wonderland Show

xxxxxxxxxxxxxxxxxxxxxxxxxxxxxx

Introducing Part 29 – The White Rabbit

C*hapter 1*

1

Hazel
The White Rabbit

"Alistair," I warned, "*no*."

He just smiled, shoving me back down onto my vanity chair. "You must if you want to enjoy the party, duchess."

I glared forward when he adjusted the collar of my shirt more over my neck.

"Is all this necessary?" I questioned as he tied the bow just under the front of my collar.

"It is a very small ball, my lady, yes, but you need social interaction."

"No, that's not what I'm saying." I glared up at him. "I'm asking why you're dressing me up like fucking *Alice in Wonderland*."

He just gazed down, adjusting my head band. "You don't like the rabbit ears, duchess?"

"Why would I like wearing a headband with obnoxious, large, animal-like ears?" I snapped.

"They're not obnoxious," he said, chuckling. "You look absolutely adorable in them, honestly. You're already look so young despite your age..." he said in a dreamy voice, "you look so innocent in these."

"I hate you," I muttered in annoyance.

He just smiled. "Duchess, I am being kind. I allowed you to say no to the make-up."

"I'm NOT having you put whiskers on me, and paint my nose *pink*," I retorted. "But I'm not fond of the ears, either, and... *can't you make this dress more comfortable?*"

"The ball is only for an hour," he said, eyes softening with his smile. "You can manage, I'm sure."

I grumbled in annoyance.

He stepped around me to catch some other stuff, and I fiddled with my thumbs before looking fully at him.

"Alistair."

He stuffed some of my belongings into a bag. "Yes, duchess?"

"I had a query about you and Agnes," I said then.

A small smile peeked on his lips, and he zipped up the bag. "Whatever's on your mind, my lady?"

I gazed over at the mirror then, staring at myself. "Did you two ever...? You know."

He stood up fully and gazed over at me, but I avoided eye contact. "I'm afraid I do not understand."

"Yes, you do," I snapped. "You understand plenty."

"I actually do not," he said then, smiling a little. "Although... judging by your reddened cheeks, I'd say you're asking something embarrassing."

I just growled low and stood, catching my cloak and storming to the door. "Whatever."

Alistair just caught my arm, reeling me to face him.

I pulled out of his grip. "Hey! What did I say about grabbing me like that?"

"My apologies, duchess," he said then, bowing slightly before standing up. "But I really must urge you to complete your thought processes." He smiled. "You claim to never feel fear, but I assure you keeping secrets is a clear sign of it."

I gritted my teeth. "What? So, you're *questioning me now*?"

"I'm merely requesting that you observe your morals," he stated then, lashes lowering. "And check them."

I just gritted my teeth.

He's pushing my self-confidence, so I'll cave. This demon.

I just stood up straight. "Are you manipulating me?"

"No, of course not." He closed his eyes kindly. "The definition of manipulation is controlling or influencing a person or situation cleverly, unfairly, or unscrupulously." He parted his lashes. "You are the leader, duchess, the king who controls her pawns. I am merely the knight awaiting command. How must I control a situation without my duchess's consent?"

"You're controlling the situation right now," I growled.

"I am merely testing your patience and slightly enabling your self-doubt," he stated then, smile widening. "I am not controlling the situation or you in any manner. Every prospect of what comes next is up to you."

I just sighed, pinching the bridge of my nose. "You really know how to smooth talk your way out of everything, don't you?"

"I am merely a demon," he said then.

I shook my head. "You always talk about only caring for me but what kind of caretaker touches and plays with his duchess?" I pointed an accusing finger at him. "And don't *ask me what I'm talking about*, because you should *know I mean something very explicit*."

He just chuckled, clearing his throat to hide it. "Duchess... if I might be frank."

I just dropped my arm. "What now?"

"Do you understand the amount of... servant romances there are? Not necessarily the dominating and submissive type, but the forbidden romance aspect that everyone falls in love with?"

I just glared. "Your point?"

"There are many servant romances out there," Alistair stated then. "Many... *many*. So... I'd say that this might be a part of the servant aesthetic? Just a tad."

I rolled my eyes and brushed off my sleeves. "You are exhausting."

"Duchess," Alistair pressed then, lashes lowering, "your question from earlier?"

I glared over at him. "I said to drop it."

He arched a brow.

I just sighed and turned away from him. "Fine. I was just asking... if you and Agnes ever had sex before."

He was silent then, but I felt his eyes burn into my back. "Are you curious about the amount of times or how I did it?"

"The amount of *times, you idiot*!" I said then, glaring over at him. "Seriously, I'm not a *pervert*."

He just smiled. "As to an estimate I'd say almost fifteen thousand times."

I gazed over at him, eyes widened in horror. "What?"

"Well," he closed his eyes kindly, "the first time I had with Agnes was when she was nineteen. She died at seventy-seven almost, and we did it almost every night. And if you do the calculations as an estimate, seventy-seven minus nineteen is fifty-eight, and there are three hundred sixty-five days in a year. If you divide the amount of days in a year by one point five—the small number of times in a year that we didn't—it would equal about fourteen thousand one hundred thirteen point three repeating."

I stared at him for a long moment. "You did all that... in your head just now?"

He gazed up at me, eyes glowing a dark red. "Duchess, I've told you many times not to underestimate me. I am a demon. You said yourself my level of intellect is higher than the smartest computer."

I just blinked and looked back at the mirror, finding my cheeks shaded a light red. "So... did... did she...?"

"Did she what?" Alistair pressed.

"Did she... like it?" I said quietly.

He chuckled a little. "My, duchess. You're always so confident and now you're blushing like you just caught a fever."

"Just answer the question!" I said, shooting him a look. "I don't need your additional torment. I get that enough as is."

He gazed up, lashes lowering. "She did."

I parted my lips and looked away.

"Why, if I may ask, do you want to know?"

I was silent.

Alistair just clasped his hands on front of him. "Duchess, may I press forward and ask what your worries are?"

I just sighed and closed my eyes tightly. "Will... will it hurt?"

"Did it hurt before?" he said then, smiling slightly. "The first time I used my fingers?"

I nodded slightly.

"Did it hurt the second time?"

I shook my head.

"Then, no," he said, lashes lowering, "if I ease you in more, it won't."

I blinked and gazed up at him. "*Ease me in*...? You mean... this whole time...?"

His smile curled further. "I don't like the idea of causing my duchess immense pain."

I blinked and stared at him for a moment, but I just gazed down and rubbed my arm nervously. "You did that with Agnes, too?"

"Yes, duchess."

"So... did it hurt her?"

"I eased her in," Alistair said, "it did not."

I just held myself, getting a sudden fluttery feeling. "Alistair, I must ask you of something."

He raised his head curiously. "My lady?"

"I know I told you to stay hidden in the shadows," I said then, gazing up. "But this task... I just... something's off about it."

He tipped his head to the side.

"Do you know the task off the top of your head?" I said then.

Alistair nodded. "There's been a series of murders around town recently. The police cannot find the culprit because they keep escaping. The police want you to find them."

I looked toward my bed. "The murder is of Count Damien the third. A very rich and powerful man whose businesses almost rival mine. He is the suspected murderer. And you see..." I looked back over at him, "the police always find a lead on the killings that run cold, so the police suspect that Damien is tapping them off in a way."

Alistair's lashes lowered. "I see."

I nodded. "Yes. A very dark manner, indeed. But" I just sighed, "I was analyzing the victims and their resemblances. It seems as if the murderer's gender of choosing is women of brunette hairstyle. They're young, ages ranging from sixteen to thirty-four, and they all suffered sexual implantation from before death and after death. Although he used protection, so no DNA was found."

"But the police know it's him," Alistair stated.

"They cannot convict what isn't there, which is the perpetrator of a rich man who has massive manipulation skills," I said then, shaking my head. "That is why I came into the situation. You know very well that I take care of these problems under the radar and make things disappear. No one asks or questions my ways."

Alistair watched me. "What is your concern, my lady?"

"I am not a hundred percent sure if Damien is the real villain," I said then, lashes lowering. "So, I must play grifter."

Alistair's lips parted. "Duchess...."

"I must," I said then, raising my voice slightly to urge him, "I must. I am eighteen, within the age range. I have black hair, matching the description of his victims. So... in order to rid of the culprit, I must be caught by them first."

"Duchess," Alistair said then, eyes glowing slightly, "I do not like the idea of this."

"I don't either, okay?" I said then, lips thinning. "Do you think I would go with this *heinous* plan and play the *kind little slut-girl* to turn some prude on? I wouldn't! It's ridiculous. I am *Hazel Damonclove*, protector of my people! I do not fall into such category as *those weaklings*."

"Then why must you go with this plan?" Alistair said then.

I sighed then, shaking my head. "I owe my people a favor after killing those teens. I told them that they were already brain-dead, but some still were not pleased."

Alistair just lowered his lashes. "Why didn't you lie to them?"

I laughed. "If they figured it out? How well would that end up?"

"Not underestimating the minds of others," Alistair said then, smiling as his eyes closed. "How very bright of you, duchess."

I just watched him. "Alistair, my request."

He gazed up then, smiling. "What would you like me to do, my duchess?"

My eyes flickered up to him. "Remember. You owe me."

"Your life is in my hands, and I can do with it as I please," he said then, smiling still. "I haven't forgotten that I owe you, duchess. That is why I'm your caretaker, is it not?"

"Good," I said then, "I told you before to stay in the shadows. Now I need you."

"You *need* me?" he echoed.

"Shut up," I said, annoyed, "I didn't finish my sentence. Don't get cocky."

He just chuckled.

"As I said, Alistair," I continued, voice tinted with irritation, "I told you before that I want you to watch me closely and make sure I'm alright. Now, I don't think that is the best idea. We have a task, and we must finish it to full completion as per the police's wishes. And this task specifically is putting my life in immediate danger."

"I'm sorry, duchess, but I must ask," he bowed in apology and stood, "you've handled murders before. Why are you so uptight and nervous about Count Damien?"

My lashes lowered, and I just stepped over to my vanity and picked up a small file I left there from last night. I picked it up and tossed it to Alistair.

He caught it.

"Look at his number-one guard's picture," I said then, "clearly. Inspect it."

He opened the file and shuffled through its contents before making it to the guard's image. He scanned it for only a second before his eyes widened just a smidge.

He then set the files on my bed and gazed over at me. "Now I am very against this task, duchess."

"Did you see his eye color?" I demanded.

"Indeed, I did. Which proves my point."

"His eyes are *red*," I explained sternly. "Red. Did you see?"

"I saw," Alistair assured me.

"Are they contacts?" I demanded.

"They are not."

"Then what is he?" I pressed.

Alistair gazed down at me then, lashes lowering. "Demon."

"Now do you understand why I'm so uptight about this?" I questioned.

"Duchess, I'm afraid I am going to press further that you do not go through with this."

"I have to."

"It impedes on your safety," he explained, "I cannot allow this."

"Alistair," I said then.

"Standing in the shadows is not good for me," he stated then. "I cannot risk you being taken."

"Alistair, *listen*," I snapped then.

He gazed down at me, lashes lowered over his angry eyes.

"I do not *want* you in the shadows anymore," I explained. "That's what I'm saying. I was trying to explain why, but apparently, you're going to freak out like a child."

He never responded, just watched me carefully.

"You are going to be my escort, and no, not the prostitute kind," I added before he could make a smart remark. "Damien's victims are all married or have a boyfriend, at the very least. He does not care about them being single or not. So, naturally, it would be fine if I came in with another man, would it not?"

Alistair just closed his eyes tightly. "His guard will know that I'm a demon."

"His guard won't care," I said then, making Alistair's lips part. "I checked Damien's files, there are not marks or tattoos on his body at all. He has not signed with the guard."

Alistair's lashes lowered. "Duchess, I am against this."

I just watched him fully. "Alistair, you will protect me. I know it."

"I will," he said then, "but I do not like the idea of you being taken by a killer, or by another *man*."

I gazed up. "You will serve as my lover at the ball, and that's final."

His lips parted then, a look of shock washing over his expression.

He stared at me, as if examining if I was serious.

But then a smile spread across his face. "My, my. You will admit to being my lover in a con against a killer, but not in real life? Why must you tease me so?"

"It's fun," I said then. "And this is a themed ball full of Damien's richest folk. I already know he's set eyes on me. I made sure to make myself known by staring at him and winking at him from far away."

"Are you trying to make me jealous?" Alistair questioned, still smirking.

"That wasn't the goal," I stated then, returning the fox smile. "But making you jealous sounds fun. Anyways, as I was saying, he invited me to this for a reason. He's planning me as his next victim. So... naturally, I am going to attend because this is a *wondrous* opportunity."

Alistair just tipped his head to the side. "Now, I'm curious. Does he know who you are?"

I shook my head, smiling. "A little makeup, putting my hair in pigtails, and dressing me in ball-like attire will make him think I'm entirely different. You have me in pigtails right now, and I have bunny ears and makeup on. He won't recognize me."

Alistair just set his finger on his chin and tipped his head to the side. "You're very coy, aren't you? You lure men with your feigned kindness."

"Everyone but *you*," I added.

"Indeed," he responded, smile widening, "you lured me in with your bite. I love your bite."

I just ignored him and continued forward. "Anyways, please let me finish, I was saying that this ball is themed *Alice in Wonderland*. You know, the book and that movie?"

"I know, duchess," he said too gently. "I am not *that* uncultured."

I continued on. "You dressed me as the white rabbit," I stated then.

He just lightly poked one of my ears, making me glare. "And you look so adorable, indeed."

"Well, I think you should be a character, too. You'd fit in better, look less suspicious."

Alistair stood fully then, tipping his head to the side. "Oh? What would I be?"

I just smiled and watched him. "I think I'd combine characters for you." I scanned his form, finding him blinking in confusion. "I think you'd make a great Mad Hatter."

He smiled then, red eyes glowing dangerously. "Oh? You think so?"

"Yes," I said then, smile sharpening, "but you're also going to wear rabbit ears out of payment for my torment today. I mean it."

He just gazed up with a dark smirk. "If it's a demand from my duchess, then I must do it. I shall be the rabbit leading you astray and also the Mad Hatter. A maniac.

"Oh, what fun."

Introducing Part 30 – Slick like Mad Hatter

C*hapter 2*

2

Alistair
Slick like Mad Hatter

"D uchess," I said then, watching Hazel as she sat next to me in the limo, "you look exhausted. Is something wrong?"

The rest of the seats were filled with our servants who insisted on coming along. Since we had little to no time to dress them, they wore their normal attire and were all mice from the beginning scene of *Alice in Wonderland*.

Hazel gazed up at me lazily as if just hearing my question, lashes lowered over tired eyes as she blinked. "What are you wearing?"

I smiled a little. "Well... you did tell me to wear bunny ears."

"I asked you to look like the Mad Hatter," she replied, annoyed. "You don't. You're wearing white bunny ears, glasses with chains that go over your ears... and your usual servant attire. What part of that fits Mad Hatter?"

"Well," I said then, smile widening, "it's in the details. You asked me to wear bunny ears, I decided to go a little farther with the glasses because bunny ears remind me of the White Rabbit. Although... the Mad Hatter is a very odd creature. Which comes his name. And I am a very odd creature, as well. So that is how I'm the Mad Hatter, my lady."

She just set her head on the back of the seat, closing her eyes. "You find a path around everything, don't you?"

My lashes lowered as my smile curled further.

"Duchess, are you a'ight?" Carter said then.

"Yeah!" Maddox said, brows drawing together. "You look amiss!"

"Do you need some water or some food?" Cammie pressed.

Scarlet just watched her nervously.

I gazed down at Hazel then, finding her lips parted as her head remained on the back of the seat. "Duchess?"

No response, but her lashes fluttered a little, telling me she was awake.

"Duchess," I said again. "*Duchess.*"

"*What?*" she snapped then, glaring slightly at me.

"What is the matter?" I said then. "You're acting off."

"I'm *tired*, you idiot," she said then, closing her eyes again. "I didn't sleep well last night."

"Oh, did duchess have another nightmare?" Scarlet said then, leaning forward. "We should maybe consult a doctor. Maybe they can help with your dreaming issues, my lady."

"*No*," Hazel said too sternly, making my lashes lower. "I'm *fine*. Just... just leave me be."

We were all silent for a moment.

Carter broke the silence then. "Okay, erm... is there somethin' I be missin'?"

We all looked over at him in question.

Yes, he was the last and final servant that was still in the cold about everything. Cammie was the first to know that Hazel was traumatized, and also the first to find out there was a romantic relationship between Hazel and I. Scarlet was the second to find out. Maddox knew duchess suffered some trauma and could clearly sense something between us after the carnival events a couple weeks ago. Carter didn't know anything.

Everyone remained silent, clearly knowing that Hazel *herself* didn't know that Cammie wasn't the only one who knew everything.

She did tell me not to tell Scarlet and Maddox about us, but I wasn't the one who told Scarlet. Cammie did. And Maddox figured it out due to duchess's psychotic break in that manor with the carnival problems.

I was just by duchess's side, obeying her command.

"You're missing nothing," Maddox lied, glaring sharply at Carter before mouthing, "*I'll tell you later*".

"Ah, I see," Carter said then, nodding and playing along. "Nightmares do happen lots. Notin' to be worried about, ey?"

Hazel remained silent.

I then turned toward her. "Duchess, there's about an hour until we get there. Would you like to sleep until then?"

She nodded, keeping her eyes closed.

"Alright, then." I smiled and caught her arm, tugging her down.

She yelped when she collided with my lap, fighting me seconds later. "Hey! Alistair! What the fuck?!"

"You need a pillow," I stated, grasping my jacket from next to me and draping it over her. "The most suitable and comfortable thing around here is my lap. We don't need another migraine occurrence from neck pain, do we? So, relax and go to sleep."

She stopped fighting then and grumbled in annoyance, dropping her hands by her sides.

I just set my hand down onto her head, starting to run my fingers along her scalp.

She eased into me then, closing her eyes tightly as she shivered a little, but I knew it was in comfort.

But I looked down, finding her lashes parted slightly as her cheeks burned a bright red.

She got embarrassed so easily. It was adorable.

After a moment, her eyes closed, and another minute after that, she was dreaming.

I smiled and looked out the window, continuing to pet her hair in hopes of keeping her asleep.

After a couple seconds, my lashes lowered. "Stop staring."

The four servants just yelped in response and scrambled around, catching an object around them and examining it.

I just looked back down at Hazel.

Ah, duchess... you cannot be resistant for long.

I will break you.

"Welcome, my lady," the man at the door said, "may I ask for your name?"

"Yuna," Hazel said then, picking up her skirts and bowing to him, "Yuna Claerita."

"Ah, Count Damien's precious guest. I am very lucky to speak to you, indeed. The pleasure it mine," the man said then, picking up her hand to lightly kiss it. He stood fully and gazed over at me, looking oddly calm despite the suspicious look I was giving him. "And you must be Lady Yuna's fiancé, erm... Edwardo, is it?"

"*Edward*," I corrected. "And yes, I am the lady's fiancé."

Hazel didn't look particularly amused, but I wasn't sure I cared.

"Who are these four?" he said then, looking at my servants.

"They're my cleaners," Hazel said, telling the truth this time, "they're here because they begged me so."

That was true, wasn't it?

Duchess, please, can we come? Please?! PLEASE?

We won't break anything, we promise!

And no explosions unless you tell me otherwise!

The man then stepped aside, letting us in the house. "The pleasure is all mine."

We all entered then, the four servants behind us following close, as well.

"Whoa," Maddox said, gazing up as his eyes shot around the room.

He watched the golden ceilings, the light, bright area with red rugs and the spiral staircase spiraling up to the top floor.

There were thousands of people in here, all talking and holding glasses of wine and champagne. Some had rabbit ears on like Hazel and I—some wore some disgusting, stupid hat to represent Mad Hatter—and others dressed as mice, turtles, and an occasional Queen of Hearts.

Hazel just continued in further into the house, and I followed.

"This is a large manor, indeed," I said then, glancing around before looking down at her. "Aren't you interested?"

"I've been in a fair share of large mansions when my father was duke," she commented then. "I could care less about flashy mansions. This one is much smaller than mine, anyway."

I continued gazing around. "Indeed, but it's so bright in here. All the walls are white and the light beams from them like the sun on a mirror. Your manor is very dark, indeed. It had white walls, but black marble flooring."

"I like it that way," she said then, stopping in the middle of the entryway, "why else would I sign a contract with a demon? You are the epitome of darkness, aren't you?"

I just scanned the room, eyes immediately locking on the guard I was warned of. I just smiled and gazed back down at her. "You make a good point, duchess."

"Far right," she warned then, "man wearing black, two guards down. See him?"

"I already spotted the demon guard, duchess."

"Well, aren't you efficient?"

"Well, if I couldn't spot an odd figure so soon, then what demon am I?"

"One that doesn't drive me insane," she retorted, lightly catching a cup of water from a person carrying a tray.

They walked off then, and she looked around a moment before swishing her water around. "I don't see Mister Killer anywhere."

"I do not either," I said then. "Are you going to drink that?" I pointed to her glass.

"Yes, clearly," she said then, giving me a look, "it's water. Chill."

"Oh, water," I said then, lashes lowering as a smile spread across my lips. "I see."

She just rolled her eyes. "So, why the name Edward?"

"Huh?"

"Your character," she explained. "The White Rabbit and Mad Hatter combination. Why name yourself Edward?"

I closed my eyes and smiled kindly. "To confuse him."

She glanced over at the guard again. "So that *is* him. Thought so."

"Indeed, he has very distinctive features. I'm not sure why you wouldn't have noticed him earlier."

"Shut up. I don't need your comments."

I gazed down at her then, finding her tipping the glass to her mouth. "Duchess, I don't really think you should—"

But it already spilled in her mouth.

As another man with empty glasses on his tray came around, I a caught one despite it being dirty.

Hazel recoiled, cheeks puffed as she lurched forward, eyes widening in horror.

I just smiled, giving her the empty cup.

She spit it out immediately, and gasped when I took the cup back, placing it on another person's tray along with her glass of "water".

"What... *was that*?" she growled in annoyance.

"Vodka," I said casually. "I smelt it a mile away. I tried to warn you."

"You could've warned me *earlier*," she snapped, setting her hands on her knees. "It tasted like rubbing alcohol mixed with rotten lime."

"Yes, indeed," I said then, pulling out a handkerchief. "Sadly, they bought the cheap alcohol." I then tipped her chin up and dabbed her lips, making her eyes widen. "It's a waste, honestly. No one would drink this."

Despite her being angry, she was now staring into my eyes, cheeks burning a bright red as I cleaned her cheeks and mouth.

I then pulled away, folding the handkerchief back into my pocket. "There. All better."

She continued staring at me, and I gazed down at her, amused.

I knew that look. She gave it every time I got close to her, and she didn't hide it well.

She snapped out of her faze for a second and looked around, clearly ignoring those feelings rising inside her. "We need to find Count Damien. Soon, too. Now that Edward is here, I don't feel comfortable staying here long."

My lashes lowered as I kept the smile.

She just started into the crowd. "Come, Alistair."

"Yes, duchess." I followed.

"Did you find anything?" Hazel said when I hopped off the second floor of the library, landing silently on the first.

"No, duchess. No evidence of his murders here."

She just pressed her finger to her chin. "I know it's him. I just have to be sure."

I watched her curiously as she remained thinking, brows drawing together in anger.

The moment I watched her expression harden, I finally spoke, "All this is getting to you, my lady. Why don't we take a break?"

"That never stopped me before," she stated then, continuing to think. "We checked his bedroom, his closet, all rooms. Well, *you* did," she added, "as per my wishes, but still found nothing. And where is Count Damien now? That's concerning me, indeed. He's nowhere in his house. Perhaps he's arriving late?"

I glanced down at her arm when I found it raising and catching her shoulder, lightly rubbing the muscle there. "If so, where would he have gone?"

My eyes flickered back up to her.

"A grocery run?" she continued, rubbing the muscle still as her face etched slightly in pain. "Is he making a large appearance like a performer or something?"

"Duchess," I said then, watching her as she gazed up, "is your shoulder bothering you?"

She looked at me for a moment before shaking her head. "No, and stop. I'm trying to think here."

"Because you're rubbing it as if it hurts," I continued.

She waved my response away. "It's just a muscle spasm. I didn't sleep good last night."

I watched her still.

"Is he a paranormal creature?" She lowered her lashes, continuing her thoughts aloud. "No, *you* would sense them. And you've only sensed Edward."

My lashes lowered.

No, I did not *only* sense Edward. I sensed two other figures, as well, but none of them were Damien himself.

Damien was not here right now. I knew that for sure.

I believed her thought of him making a big entrance deemed fit. He was the selfish type. It seemed fit for something he would do.

I then stepped over to her.

But it didn't matter right now. As long as if he wasn't here, then she was safe and there was nothing to be done. She needed to ease her mind a bit and stop ignoring her pain.

I stopped next to her, finding her murmuring possible outcomes and thinking this through. But I caught her arm, and she blinked, gazing up at me.

"Duchess," I said gently, "he is not here. His form is not here. Which means there is no job to be done, and you need to relax a bit."

She just pursed her lips, looking a tad nervous.

I pulled her forward. "Come. Follow me."

She listened, stepping after me as I made it to an empty fireplace in the middle of the room, and I guided her to sit on the couch in front of it—clearly a reading couch—and I went back behind her.

I put my hands on her shoulders, deepening my fingers slightly into her skin and feeling her wince. But I gently started massaging, and she tensed, clearly not liking the feeling.

"Untense your muscles," I told her, "and it won't hurt as much."

She listened—surprisingly—and relaxed into the back of the couch.

Her face etched slightly as I kneaded her shoulders and the base of her neck, but she looked a more relieved now.

This moment went on for about three minutes, and I kept going until she seemed half-asleep, finally letting go. "Better?"

She nodded lazily, parting her lashes.

I just lowered my face inches to hers, watching her become a little flushed but lesser than normal.

I ran my fingers along her chin, caressing the skin lightly before tipping her chin further back.

And I clasped my lips with hers.

She moaned in response, clearly half-asleep still because she didn't catch my shoulders or neck this time.

But she was giving in, raising her head so she could get a little closer.

I deepened the kiss, pressing her a little into the couch as her eyes squeezed shut tighter and she moaned a little more.

But my eyes flew open, burning a bright red, and I stood up quicker than light, holding my arm out and shielding her immediately.

Hazel sat up then, clearly out of shock, and gazed around me.

Her stance stiffened.

Augustus stood by the latter to the top floor of the library, smiling creepily as my eyes narrowed.

Another man landed next to him as if falling from the ceiling, one with long, blonde hair and thickened, long lashes. He wore a pair of harry-potter glasses, and his teeth sharpened into a grin.

"Hello, *Allie*," the red-haired man said, voice chipper and oddly squeaky; like a grown man going through puberty. He just set his hand on his hip, winking. "Remember me?"

My lashes lowered, and Hazel stared at them in confusion. "Benji Thornheart," I said then, standing up straighter, "how could I forget the likes of you?"

"*Benji* Thornheart?" Hazel said then. "You mean that pervert of a fallen that Agnes despised beyond belief? The one who always tried to hook up with you?"

Alistair sighed. "That's him."

"*Oh*!" Benji said then, practically steaming as hearts grew in his eyes. "You thought of me every *day*, haven't you? Ever since out *sinful* departing! Oh, how I missed my *Allie*!"

"I am not... *yours*," I said then, lashes lowering in annoyance. "I just remember you being a nuisance, that's all."

"Oh, so cooooold!" he said then, wrapping his arms around himself and shaking his body. "And the bunny ears so adorable! How alluring!"

"How... distracting," Hazel said then, face etched in disgust.

"What do you want now?" I said to him. "Didn't I tell you to leave me and Hazel alone?"

"I missed you so *much*, though!" he said, winking at me. "You missed me, too, huh?"

"Not particularly," I said, sighing.

"Oh, you *liar*," Benji said then, swiping his hand at me. "Typical Alistair, loves to play hard to get."

We all just stared at him in annoyance.

"Well..." Hazel said then, breaking the silence, "now that *this* nuisance had his introduction, why don't you tell us why you're here, Augustus?"

"*Nuisance*?" Benji echoed. "How could you say such things?! I traveled so far and mighty to see Allie's lovely face again! My, oh, my how I missed him! His cruel, joking features and his *demonic* stare." He chuckled giddily and wrapped his arms around himself. "Just like old times, hmm? I'm so, very jealous! How could you steal such a treasure?"

"Well, my lady, I couldn't help but overhear that another demon would be in play tonight," Augustus said as Benji kept going on in the background. "You see... I hear a lot of things, indeed."

"Oh, I know," Hazel said then, setting her chin on the back of the chair. "You always come at such inconvenient times. Now, if I may ask, who is 'the father'?"

"And continuously ignore me right *now*!" Benji said then, going on still but we ignored him. "Ah-*ha-ha-ha-ha-ha*!"

"I'm sorry I am not allowed to give answers to you, my lady," Augustus said then. "This part is crucial in my working environment."

"Wait... did you say, '*my lady*'?" Benji said then, making my lashes lower.

"Now, now, Benji," Augustus said, "you mustn't be so oblivious. Be kind to the young duchess. She may only be eighteen, but she's still considered superior to us."

Benji's eyes bugged out. "*Really*? That's very confusing."

"*You're* very confusing," Hazel retorted. "And irritating. Can you go now? Alistair and I have business to attend to."

"Ah, yes..." Augustus said, "the kissing."

"No, not the *kissing*, you blundering *idiot*!" she retorted defensively, sitting up now as I smiled. "I have a job to do other than *snogging*! How *dare* you insult me so?! I am not a needy weakling like other *earthlings*!"

"Ah, the defensiveness," Augustus said, giggling. "Just like Agnes."

"Wait! Hold on!" Benji said frantically. "Kissing?! This is entirely new to me!"

We all gazed over at him in annoyance, but Hazel was blushing now.

"You didn't see that?" Augustus said. "That was five minutes ago. Well... I do suppose you *just got here*."

"I thought you'd save yourself for *me*, Allie!" Benji argued, looking entirely hurt. "How could you go for some over-the-counter girl!"

My lashes lowered, and I felt Hazel fuming from behind me.

Three.

Two.

One.

"First! I am not an OVER-THE-COUNTER GIRL!" she yelled then, face burning brighter. "I am Hazel Damonclove! Duchess Damonclove! You will treat me as such! Second! I was caught in the heat of the moment! Alistair is being a jerk, that's all!"

Now, she was continuing in the background.

"Wait..." Benji said then, tipping his head to the side, "Damonclove? That seems oddly familiar."

"Don't you remember the little Agnes girl?" Augustus said then. "She was fifteen when you first met. Don't you remember?"

Benji thought for the moment, but he then smiled. "Oh, yes. That's where Allie first met me!" He squealed like a child.

I just lowered my lashes in annoyance, still hearing Hazel yelling behind me. "You truly are bothersome."

"You *love* that of me."

"I despise you, Benji."

Hazel fumed then. "Are you even *listening*?!"

"Ah, no, sorry, my lady," Augustus said then. "We were side-tracked, I'm afraid."

"Well, I'm *sorry* to ruin your reunion, but we really should get going," Hazel said then, tone sharp.

Benji examined her for a moment. "Wait... you look familiar."

She gazed up then, annoyed.

He stared at her for a moment before his eyes widened. "Oh, my. *Agnes*? You're still alive? How is that even possible?! Didn't you sign the contract ages ago?!"

Hazel looked taken aback for a moment.

"She is not Agnes," I said then, gazing up in annoyance. "I'm sure the pigtails tell you that much. Agnes wasn't one to dress like that. She hated looking childish. I'm sure you can remember the time we forced her into that maid outfit."

"Oh, I can very much," Benji said then, chuckling. "Best day of my life. What else can a fallen ask for?" He then looked down at Hazel. "You look a lot like her, though. And you're in the same family?"

Her eyes narrowed in annoyance.

"Hazel, here, has Agnes's soul," Augustus said then, making all of us look over to find his smile wide. "It has transferred to her."

Benji looked back down, smirking. "And the covered eye and *everything*. So alike."

"Excuse me, but I must stop this gawking and continue searching for Count Damien," Hazel said then, standing.

"Oh, you won't find him," Augustus said then, making both of us stop.

"What?" Hazel said then. "Why?"

"The count won't show himself until midnight," Benji stated then, smirking. "He is planning a big show for us all. Why do you think I'm here?"

"To eye-rake Alistair, I thought," Hazel said sarcastically. But she continued, "Are you suggesting that you both are here because there is a massive patch of deaths happening?"

Benji just winked. "You got it, Allie Stealer!"

Her brow twitched in annoyance.

"And, what about *you*?" I said then, looking over at Augustus. "Why are you here?"

"I just want to enjoy the show," he responded, lashes lowering. "Is that too much to ask?"

I then glanced over at Hazel with a question in my eyes and found her looking at me with the same query, and then we both looked at Augustus.

Hazel just turned and started to the door. "Come, Alistair."

I bowed. "Duchess." And I followed, pushing my glasses higher on my nose.

But we both heard Benji chuckle from behind us. "You signed with her, too, Alistair? My, you must really want her blood, don't you?"

A smile crossed my face. "You have no idea. And for different reasons, nonetheless."

We only made it to the corridor outside Count Damien's library before Hazel caught my arm and tugged me the opposite direction.

I just followed. "Duchess, you can just tell me to follow you."

She was silent, but I could see her stance start trembling.

My lashes lowered.

But we entered another room, and she slammed the door shut behind us. "Are they following us?" she demanded.

"They are not," I said.

"Is there anyone in here?" she demanded. "It's dark."

"No, duchess."

She then pulled me further in the room, breathing uneasily before she tripped over something and fell.

I caught her at an instant.

When I lifted her back on her feet, I looked around the blackened room before gazing down at her. "Duchess, you look troubled. What's wrong?"

She had her arm clutched in her hand, trembling still. "Alistair, something's not right."

"Duchess, you're shaking," I said then, stepping over to her and catching her arms to comfort her. "Do you sense something?"

She nodded, gazing around. "These people... they're going to die. All of them." She breathed uneasily. "He's going to kill them all."

"That bothers you?" I said then.

"Of course, it bothers me, you *dimwit*!" she yelled then, making my lashes lower. "How would it not?!"

"Is that all?" I said then.

"Of *course* it is," she said then, glaring at me. "Do you want *more*? Is this not *enough* for you?"

"I'm sorry, my lady, but I must comment." I gazed down at her, red eyes glowing slightly. "You've seen people die before, and this bothers you? All of them are rich and heartless, too. Why do you care?"

"But I have the opportunity to save them."

"You have in the past," I continued, "and yet Madam Deneise still died. You let it go. And this looks as if it's triggering your trauma. You're clutching arm with the scarring. It suggests something, doesn't it?"

She gazed down at her am and let it go, stepping backwards. "I don't like it when you question me."

"Duchess," I said then, watching her carefully, "you're hiding something from me."

"Alistair, just *stop*," she snapped then, making my lashes lower. "I told you to *stop*."

I silenced then, listening to her wishes.

She was quiet, too, but eventually stepped backwards into the darkness, turning and making her way forward.

I watched as she tripped over something again, but I was there within seconds, catching her.

She gazed up hazily when I lifted her back onto her feet, and she continued forward, me following close behind.

She stopped by the window with moonlight beaming through the closed drapes, and she drew a curtain back, blue eye lighting up with the moon's glow.

She stared outside for a moment before closing the curtain and turning back away.

Paranoia? No... something else.

She continued further in the room before she tripped again. I was there, catching her.

She breathed uneasily.

"Duchess, I don't want you getting hurt," I said then, scooping her up. "So, I'll just carry you to a couch."

I continued further into the room before setting her down onto a couch, and she stared off into the distance when I looked down at her dress.

"It came undone," I said more to myself.

I knelt down then and adjusted the ribbon on her collar, slipping it through itself and pulling it back into a bow.

Hazel just dropped off the couch.

I moved to catch her before I foresaw what she was doing.

She fell onto my lap, knocking me onto my knees, and threw her arms around me, burying her face in my shoulder.

Shock rattled through me, but eventually it fell, and I wrapped an arm around her, lightly setting my hand on her head to run down her strands of black hair.

"Duchess..." I said gently, "...I need to know if you're alright. Are you hurting anywhere?"

She kept herself buried against me but shook her head.

I continued to run my fingers through her hair, scanning all circumstances of this being related to her trauma.

But it clicked, and I closed my eyes.

Of course. I saw it before but didn't acknowledge it.

"We can go home," I suggested.

She shook her head, voice muffled in my chest. "Just... give me a minute."

I set my cheek on her head and gently rubbed her back. "I'll give you an hour."

She was silent for a moment. "Alistair."

"Yes?"

"Edward is here," she said quietly, "Augustus is, too. So is Benji. Edward and Augustus in the same place... a large amount of deaths happening... Do you understand what this means?"

"Yes," I said gently.

"The father is up to this," she said quietly.

"Duchess, why are you so weary about Count Damien?" I said then.

She suddenly started shaking and buried her face further into my neck, fisting my shirt in her hands.

It clicked again.

I just closed my eyes, continuing to rub her back. "I understand. You don't have to tell me."

She just buried herself further against me, breathing shakily.

"It's okay," I said then, continuing to soothe her. "I won't let him take what's mine."

And making you afraid was his first mistake.

Introducing Part 31 – Dark Smile

C*hapter 3*

3

Hazel
Dark Smile

"**D**o you sense anything?" I asked Alistair as we walked around the manor together.

"I do not, your grace," he answered, staying close by my side. "It seems as if the demonic guard has not left his post."

We both gave Edward a cautious glance before continuing into the crowd.

"This unsettles me," I said, voice low. "What is he planning to do with all these people?"

"My main guess is that the father is behind this," Alistair stated honestly. "So, my direct assumption is that all these people are his next creatures."

I just sighed, something cold consuming me. "His victims are mainly women... which doesn't connect well, does it?"

"It could be a personal preference," Alistair said then. "He could be a killer and also be working for 'the father'."

"I hate to praise you, but perhaps you are right," I said then, thinking this thoroughly. "Which is nothing new, really."

A small smile formed on his lips.

"Don't get cocky," I snapped then, looking around the crowd. "That wasn't a compliment."

"Being right is an insult?" Alistair said then. "Even when you directly stated that you hated praising me? How confusing."

I just ignored him. "I see no suspicious figures other than Edward standing guard. Augustus and Benji look like they're having fun and searching through the food table." I paused then, blinking. "Wait... where are my servants? I think I lost them a while ago."

I glanced around then, immediately gazing up at Alistair to find his eyes closed and the smile still curling his lips.

But I looked behind him.

My lashes lowered when a beat of sweat slipped down my cheek.

"Oh, *hya mister carpenter*!" Carter said, slurring his words while karate chopping Maddox.

"Ey! I like my hair the way it is!" Maddox said then, slurring his words as well when he shrank back.

"Both of you," Scarlet said then, also sounding drunk while shoving them away, "shut your mouths. I have a headache!"

Cammie waddled around them, tripping over nothing and falling.

I just closed my eyes tightly, the veins on my neck throbbing. "Idiots got drunk the moment they got here, didn't they?"

"I insisted that I'd pick the staff, duchess," Alistair said then, sounding slightly amused. "But you went for those wrecks."

"At least they're good bodyguards," I said then, starting back into the crowd as Alistair followed me. "Any other senses?"

"Ah, no..." Alistair said then, "I don't sense Damien anywhere near here. And as for paranormal creatures, those three nuisances are still here, no new ones."

I looked around. "I see. Very curious, indeed."

We were both silent for a moment.

"Alistair," I said then, making him gaze up curiously.

"Duchess?" he said then.

"Do something for me, would you?" I said then, gazing up at him. "Figure out what Count Damien is up to. Search the house, closed places. Anything, really."

His lashes lowered then. "Duchess, I do not feel comfortable doing this with Edward near."

"It should only take you a couple seconds," I stated then, lashes lowering. "Be a good demon and hurry up, would you? Go find out. I mean it. And," I added, putting a finger up, "don't tell me 'your survival is at risk' because Edward doesn't seem interested right now. He hasn't glanced at me once."

Alistair sighed then, closing his eyes in annoyance. "Very well."

"You have five seconds," I stated. "This time I expect you to take five seconds rather than twenty minutes."

He smiled slightly.

I pointed a finger up. "Starting now. Go."

He suddenly vanished.

One.

Two.

Three.

Four.

Five.

He reappeared again, making me gaze up numbly.

"Well?" I said then.

He smiled slightly, but his eyes were burning in anger. "I figured it out."

I arched a brow.

He just caught my arm and pulled me to another hallway, and I stumbled a little when he tugged me into a room and closed the door behind us.

I gazed up, brushing off my bandaged arm before looking up at him fully.

He set his back against the door. "It isn't good."

I just lowered my lashes. "Enlighten me."

"The killings are not connected to 'the father' in the slightest. Edward is here because he knew *you* would be here, and Augustus, as well. They were probably bored and were seeking entertainment. Benji is here because there is about to be a series of killings within the night, and he likes witnessing murder." He gazed up with dark eyes. "I found Damien's charges, but there isn't enough to convict him."

My lashes lowered. "What are his charges?"

"Murder one," Alistair said then, looking grim. "For fifty victims."

My eyes widened then, breaths stilling.

"According to his file," Alistair said, "the police suspect that he's a serial killer. He kidnaps women by luring them in with charm, and then ties them down, kills them, and then has sexual intercourse with them."

I just set my finger on my chin, thinking thoroughly despite the bile rising in my throat. "Serial killer, huh? That explains it. But he keeps tapping the police off which is why they cannot convict him; he's tampering with governmental documents. But still... what is he planning to do with all these people here then?"

"I'm afraid I do not know," Alistair stated, "his plans are all in his head, it seems. I'm not very sure if I can find evidence of his plans tonight. Although," he added, making me gaze up, "judging by the times of the fifty murders, they were getting closer and closer together through time. Years apart, then months, then weeks, then days. So, I suspect that he's planning a mass murder... a big finish."

I just stared at him for a moment, body growing cold. "No... no that doesn't fit him."

Alistair blinked then, brows drawing together. "Duchess, you're saying that as if you know him."

Another cold pain struck me, but I attempted to ignore it. "I know, but still... something's amiss." I then gazed up to find him watching me suspiciously. "Alistair... are you a hundred percent sure that he has no other victims currently?"

"I am not," he said then. "He could have a thousand women hidden somewhere; I do not know."

I swallowed something hard and tapped my chin. "Then we still must go through with the plan. I have to find those women."

"Isn't there another way, duchess?" Alistair urged then, voice dark. "I still am weary about your capturing."

I just closed my eyes tightly. "If you found out where they are, then I would say we wouldn't. But you just told me there was no evidence of his plans. The only thing you would be able to find would be documents to a cabin or something, a place he owns, but it's a high possibility he burned the documents or erased the file. Depending on what sites it's on."

Alistair was silent then. "Duchess."

"We have to save those women, Alistair," I stated then, shaking slightly. "Don't you understand? They could be going through hell right now. And Damien has sights for me... if I convince him to take me, then maybe the people in this manor will be saved. He would have different priorities."

Alistair watched me suspiciously.

I felt shivers start racking through me, my blood burning and cooling, boiling inside me.

Fear.

I knew why I was afraid. It was because I knew Damien. I knew him personally.

And I didn't particularly like him or what he did to me.

Alistair just stepped over to me, lightly catching my hand and making my head shoot up.

He knelt down and kissed my knuckles. "I do whatever you wish, duchess. This is your game, after all."

My brows drew together, and he stood back up, still holding my hand.

"But first, we must stop the shaking," he said then, pulling me forward until I collided with his chest.

I gasped a little at the action, but he just scooped me up and carried me further into the darkness of the room.

I gazed up at him hazily, only seeing the moonlight reflecting off him in a silhouette, and the red in his irises glowed like a lamp despite his shadowed form.

He then settled down beside a wall, holding me in his lap as I sat against him, resting my head on his shoulder.

"I know how to ease your mind," Alistair said then, lightly running his index finger along my stomach.

I sucked in a breath, closing my eyes tightly.

"I just have to distract you for a bit," he stated then, letting his finger fall further... and further down.

He slipped it under me, but not inside this time.

Instead, he started rubbing a sensitive spot... a spot no one had ever touched before.

I closed my eyes tightly, holding back a moan.

"Focus on it rather than the situation," he said gently. "I will make you forget everything."

He then set his hand fully on it, starting to caress a little harder.

I whimpered, nails digging into his shoulders.

"This is a sensitive spot, indeed," he stated then, sounding amused. "You're all flushed."

"Shut up..." I said then, shivering a little as he rubbed faster.

I tipped my head back, mouth dropping open as warmth flooded me, pooling deeper and deeper... until...

I cried out, but Alistair just covered my mouth, holding my face to his neck as he kept rubbing me down there.

He was clearly riding it out.

He kept his fast pace, letting the orgasm go deeper, and deeper.

Until I grew incredibly sensitive, almost like he dropped hot wax on me, and I lurched forward.

He pulled his hand away then, making my eyes close tightly as I breathed for a moment.

He let go of my mouth and held me against him, gently rubbing my arm in soothing up-and-down motions.

"That was fast," he said then.

"Shut up," I hissed. "I don't need your infuriating comments."

"Perhaps not." He just caught my shoulder and pulled me against him, helping me tuck my face into his neck as he held me tightly. "But, alas, you still need *me*."

I never responded, just kept my position.

I didn't know how he always did it, but... every time he did this, I felt so calm and at ease. It was like I had a euphoric high and now I was stuck in a numb highness... and exhausting highness.

Alistair brushed his hand down my hair. "You're mine."

I just opened my eyes softly, a smile peeking through my lips. "I'm contracted to you, yes. My life is yours."

The contract I signed with him. He would remain my caretaker, he would act as my servant, follow my demands, protect me from harm. In exchange, my life belonged to him, and the moment my wish was granted, he could drop the servant act and drink my blood.

Although, he was no longer contracted to kill me, he could do what he wished with me.

He could slaughter me.

He could devour my life.

Or he could save me.

And he could love me.

It was his decision, and I had no say in whether or not he chose to kill me. This was a tad unsettling, but I signed the contract with him knowing the risks.

I accepted the risks.

Alistair could tear my soul into pieces. Stab me and saw me in half. Slaughter me or suffocate me. Smother me or poison me.

Or he could love me, save me.

I accepted that the moment I signed with him.

After a minute or so, he finally broke the silence.

"There's twenty minutes until the Count comes back to start the show. In the meantime. I only ask you stay here with me until then."

I never replied, although my answer was clear with my lack of movement.

I would stay.

Introducing Part 32 – Dancing with the White Rabbit

C*hapter 4*

4

Hazel

Dancing with The White Rabbit

"Welcome to my manor!" Count Damien yelled into the room, making me stiffen as Alistair remained at my side. "I apologize for my late appearance, but I had some preparations to make! Everyone enjoys a good show, correct?"

The audience yelled in excitement, making my lashes lower as something cold consumed me.

"Alright, well the show will begin here in a couple minutes," Damien said then, clapping. "For now, enjoy the lovely couple dance."

Music blasted through the room again, and I gazed up as he walked toward the staircase, my eyes following him closely.

"Now's my chance," I said then, stepping forward.

But I stopped in my tracks when around fifty couples held each other and spun around, swaying with one another with their hands on their backs.

I tried to step around them, but another couple stopped in my way, swirling around.

I gazed back up at Damien, finding him immersed in conversation with one of his people.

"Goddamn it," I murmured, "we're running out of time."

Alistair stepped forward then, making my gaze snap to his.

He just smiled, eyes glowing under the lighting. "My young Duchess, there's only one way toward him. We must get through the crowd as average as we can."

My eyes narrowed at him.

He just bowed slightly and held out his hand, lips curling into a smirk. "Duchess... may I have this dance?"

I gave him a warning look, but accepted it, knowing that this was the only way we could cut across.

I caught onto his hand, and he pulled me toward him at an instant.

I gasped when I collided with his chest, but he just caught onto my hand and pushed it out, setting his other on my back.

Heat shot through me at his touch.

"Now," he said, amused, "let's dance."

He then pulled us into the crowd, making me stumble a little, but he swayed with me.

I gazed up at him then, eyes widened as my cheeks heated.

He had his eyes on me, glowing a bright red, and his lashes lowered when I kept staring at him.

I watched my dress swirl around with us at every sway he spun us in, and I felt my pigtails blow with our movement, splaying across my chest, and slipping down my back, onto his hand.

But my eyes were locked on his, finding the demonic glow still simmering in his gaze, darkening, waiting.

He kept spinning us, the smile creeping up higher as he read my embarrassed expression.

I nearly cursed at myself for not hiding it, but... I was too mesmerized to care.

But we finally made it to the other side, and Alistair let go of my back, spinning me one last time before releasing me forward.

I felt my dress swirl again when I stopped, wrapping around me with the force and releasing, but I just set my hands at my sides, gazing up at him.

He just bowed, setting his hand on his chest before standing up straighter.

But I suddenly heard a voice from behind me:

"Oh, my... is that who I think it is?"

I stilled then, breaths shaking when I recognized Damien's dark, deep tone.

I turned then, forcing a smile as Damien stepped toward me.

"Yuna Claerita," Count Damien said then, raising his hands as an introduction. "It's been a while since I've seen you."

I glanced to my right then, finding Alistair's form gone, so I turned back toward the killer.

I curtsied then. "It has, Sir Damien. How I've missed you so."

He just tipped my chin up, making my eyes widen as I sucked in a breath. "Please," he said then, eyes glowing dangerously, "just Damien to you, Sweetheart."

I felt a shiver of disgust roll through me but did my best to hide it. "O—of course, D—Damien."

He smiled and released me but set his hand on my back. "I didn't think I would find you here."

"Well... here I am."

"You brought an escort?" Damien said then, glancing to where Alistair originally stood. "Is he your boyfriend?"

I attempted to look grim or unimpressed. "Yes, unfortunate-ly."

Damien just chuckled. "Ah, that's a shame. He left you at the alter, didn't he? How depressing."

I gazed up then, continuing to play the game I started. "Sir Damien, if I may ask... why are you so interested in me?"

He gazed down then, lashes lowering. "You're a very pretty girl, Yuna. Very beautiful, indeed." He trailed his fingers up my back, and I clenched my teeth as another wave of disgust filled me.

"I think..." he said then, "I should take you away from here. Right now. What do you think?"

I pretended to look curious despite the thought of *horary!* screaming through me. "What about the show you planned?"

He just smiled, eyes still glowing dangerously. "It can hold. I must impress my lady friend first, no?"

I felt a bead of sweat slide down my temple. "Where would you like to take me?"

His smile sharpened a little, holding out his hand. "It's a surprise."

I just caught onto his hand with no hesitation, and he smiled, pulling me toward the staircase.

As we walked up, I glanced around to spot Alistair, but he was nowhere to be seen.

Edward was still in his position, glancing up at me with a dark smile.

I ignored him, though, gazing back up as we entered the top floor, and Damien pulled me to the right, down a hall.

But we entered a room not-far ahead, and he closed the door behind me.

A bedroom. A master bedroom.

I gazed up then, a tad nervous, but he just let go of my hand and stepped over to the bedside.

I watched as he picked up a bottle of liquor and a scotch glass, and I watched as he poured the liquor into a glass.

"Oh," I said then, laughing nervously, "I'm underage."

He smiled when he gazed up at me, just finishing pouring the second glass. "When has that stopped naughty girls like you before?"

I swallowed down nausea as he stepped over and handed me a glass, and I hesitantly took it.

It was poisoned. I was not to drink this.

He stepped to the side, pulling out a small handkerchief from his suit pocket and waving it out. "You're looking at it as if you fear it's drugged."

"I have to be cautious," I stated kindly, gazing up with a forced smile. "I apologize. Maybe we can do this without the liquor?"

He just kept his handkerchief out and closed his eyes while his smile sharpened. "I apologize, my lady, but moving you is better when you're drugged."

My eyes widened in horror.

I immediately moved to escape.

But he just slammed the handkerchief over my mouth, making me cry out.

The second I breathed it in, my world tilted, growing dark and foggy as if my sight were faltering.

Damien just kept the cloth to my mouth. "It wasn't the drink that was poisoned, I'm afraid. Every girl falls for this trick."

And I fell.

Introducing Part 33 – Beheaded by Red

C*hapter 5*

5

Hazel
Beheaded by Red

It was dark.

I couldn't see a thing.

I stared into the darkness, breaths shaking as the cloth in my mouth dampened with my saliva, and it tightened around my ears, making my breaths shake.

It was dark, but... I was blindfolded.

I could feel it tickling my lashes, and I kept blinking to rid of the feeling.

My hands were tied behind my back, my legs tied down, too, but by the position I was in, I could tell I was in a chair.

I struggled against the bindings harder, but suddenly I felt a cold hand running along my cheek.

I froze.

"Little girl," Damien said quietly, making my breaths shake, "did you really think you could fool me?"

He ripped the blindfold off, making me cry out through the gag, but he just stepped back, chuckling.

A sudden light burned my eyes, a large, white one... a spotlight.

I gazed around then, eyes widening when I found a crowd of people gathered under a stage I was on.

Every person wore a masquerade mask of some sort, or some kind of blindfold that they could see through.

I gazed down then, finding myself in the same dress, same outfit, but my eye patch was gone.

I closed my eye then, hoping no one noticed the mark inside it.

If only they could remove the gag... I could call Alistair.

I struggled harder, fear burning through me like fire.

Damien just stepped over, gesturing to me. "This girl is a perfect description of criminal. She was my first child I took, an alone child with a broken eye. Perfect for my freak show, huh?"

My eyes widened then, and I felt my bones chill.

He knew... it was me the whole time?

"She was the one I tried to sell to a wonderful family who could have some good use for a broken thing like her. But she murdered all of my people after throwing a tantrum at the stage." He gazed down at me then, eyes darkening as my breaths shook. "You're a liar, aren't you, little Damonclove?"

I struggled harder.

"As you know," he said then, gazing up at the crowd, "this stage is for fixing misfit behaviors. Murdering the ones who cause me anger. And... this little bitch was so, *so* ungrateful after I took her in. She deserves every speck of this."

I watched as he stepped over to a tray on the side table, and he picked up a thin, small scalpel.

My eyes widened in horror, and I shook my head frantically.

He just stepped over to me carefully, and I fought against the bindings harder.

Alistair? Where was he? Why hadn't he intervened yet?

My body grew cold, bones chilling, every aspect of me burning and freezing at the same time.

Damien just stopped in front of me, making my blood run cold.

He knelt down, a small smile forming on his lips. "You thought you could trick me, didn't you?" I winced when he ran the tip of the scalpel along my chest. "Yuna Claerita," he scoffed, "dumb girl. You were my first victim, Hazel. Why did you think I wouldn't recognize you?"

He lightly scraped my collarbone with the blade, making me wince when I felt my skin open slightly, blood spilling down the front of my chest.

Alistair... *Alistair*!

If only I could call him aloud... he would come right away no matter what problems he was facing.

"You caused me great misfortune," Damien said darkly as I tried to remain calm. "I think I might give you an even greater death than your parents. They fought back, too, you know. Very well, indeed."

My eyes widened in horror, bones chilling.

So, my parents murder... and my kidnapping were connected? He murdered them just so he could take me and sell me off to some rich asshole?

I closed my eyes tightly as he ran the blade on the already open wound, making me whimper.

But he gazed up, lightly undoing my gag and letting it fall.

I gasped for air, breath shaking.

Damien just smiled darkly. "Any last words?"

My head shot up then, eyes shrinking in horror. "ALIS-TAIR!"

Damien shrank back then, brows drawing together when he glanced at the crowd.

He then looked back at me, smile widening. "Your caretaker's name? How unfortunate. You've become very close to him, haven't you?" He then raised the blade again, making my eyes widen. "Too bad I'm going to screw up that pretty face of yours. Jab both eyes, watch you bleed out and beg for mercy."

He started toward me then, smile widening like the psycho he was.

I just smirked, making him freeze. I chuckled darkly, tipping my head back a little as I stared at the ceiling. "Too bad your crowd isn't here to watch your show anymore."

He blinked then and looked toward the audience.

He dropped the scalpel. "What...?"

Every guest was scattered across the floors, blood slipping out from their necks, eyes, noses, and ears... some pierced with freshly washed knives, others with their heads spun backward, and the last with their ribs caved in with in-human force.

"What...?" he said then, glancing around nervously. "How did...?"

But a voice came from behind him:

"I apologize, sir, but my duchess is late to bed."

Damien froze then, eyes rounding when he stood up straighter.

He spun around, breaths shaking when his eyes locked on Alistair.

He who stood at the end of the stage, eyes glowing their demonic red as his entire body remained a shadow; the only thing visible were his irate gaze and his shark-like smile.

"You..." Damien said then, pupils shrinking, "*what are you*?!"

"Me?" Alistair said then. "Why I am a servant. I take care of my duchess. And *you*, are a dead man, I'm afraid."

Damien just stared in horror, taking a couple steps back.

"I'm done with this game," I said then, brows drawing together as I fought the dark pain consuming me. "I'm tired and in *pain* and SUFFERING! *I want him to die*! *JUST KILL HIM ALREADY!*"

Alistair vanished.

One second passed.

And the next, Damien lurched forward, eyes widening when something tore through his chest all the way through his back.

My eyes widened then, blood splattering on my face.

Alistair stood on the other side of Damien, his hand piercing completely through Damien's chest, bursting a massive hole as if he was torn through by a missile. I could even see Alistair's chest through the gap, as well.

Alistair pulled his hand back, and Damien fell forward, collapsing onto the ground, deceased.

I watched as Alistair stood up straighter and pulled off his reddened glove, tossing it aside.

I breathed shallowly.

He just stepped over to me and knelt down, his demonic-like appearance gone and replaced with his normal attire.

I watched hazily as he undid my ties and let them fall.

He pulled me onto him, and I closed my eyes tightly, breath shaking when I wrapped my arms around him.

"I could've died..." I whispered uneasily. "Where were you?"

"I won't let you die," Alistair promised. "I would've come if you called me or not, either way, I would still be here."

I just held onto him tightly. "You should've come sooner."

"I apologize, duchess," he said quietly, "Edward sought fit to attack me right as I attempted to follow you. I have reason to believe this was a scheme of his to kill you, and then drink your blood once you died."

I stared down at his chest then, lashes lowering.

"Duchess..." Alistair said then, tone dark, "why didn't you tell me that Damien was the one you wanted killed? That he was the finishing to your wish?"

"I never knew his name, only his face," I said then, the cold swelling deeper when I gazed down at his corpse. "I knew his face when this task was assigned to us. But... I didn't know how to tell you. I guess I hoped I could spend a little more time with you before my side of the contract vanishes." I was silent for a moment before realizing, "You killed him."

Alistair was silent for a moment. "Indeed, I did."

"So... does that mean... that this is the end?"

"No, my lady," he said then, letting go and watching me with dark eyes, "I can do with your life as I wish now, remember?"

"Yes, but you are no longer bound to me," I said then, eyes darkening. "You're set free."

Alistair just smiled, making me blink. "When have I ever wanted to be free? What if I want to be chained? What if I want to be bound to you for eternity?"

I stared for a moment, eyes darkening. "You don't want to be set free?"

He just smiled. "What do you think?"

"But my life still belongs to you."

"Indeed, it does." He gazed up then, smile widening. "I like playing caretaker. I wouldn't mind it if I spend it a lifetime with you."

Something inside me heated, and I felt the cold wash away. "You... *like* playing caretaker?"

"Why else do you think I'm obsessed with being your servant?" he said then, chuckling. "Cooking you healthy meals, making sure you get to bed on time, helping you pick out clothes. I'm overconfident with it."

"You're overconfident with *everything*," I retorted.

He just smiled.

I then sighed and stood, and he stood with me.

"I want to go home," I told him. "Now."

He just bowed. "At once, duchess."

Introducing Part 34 – Little Bunny

C*hapter 6*

6

Alistair
Little Bunny

"Duchess," I said as I entered her study, "come, now. It's time for bed."

"One second, it's getting good," she said then.

I gazed down then, finding her sitting on the floor by a bookshelf on the wall, and she was nose-deep into a novel, a newer-looking one at that.

I then blinked at her attire.

She changed from her dress and was now wearing a blue sweater and no pants, but had her underwear on, of course. But what *really* bothered me was... the bunny ears that were still on her head, twitching a little but I knew it was the wind from the window.

I stepped over to her then, setting a tray of her milk and honey down. "Duchess."

"Shhh!" she said then, pushing her face further in the book. "Almost *done*!"

I looked to the cover then, finding a girl there wearing a bright pink shirt that showed her stomach—blue-ish white hair covering one eye—and a small boy stood next to her with a petty grin—yellow, spikey hair blowing in the non-existent wind as his loose tie and black overcoat glowed with him.

A comic?

No, it was like a comic, but the correct term would be "manga".

"Is that the manga about the demon boy and the angel girl?" I said then, stepping over to her. "You're already on book thirteen? My, you're a fast reader, aren't you?"

Hazel ignored me as I knelt down behind her, reading it from behind her back.

It was a scene where the blonde girl—the angel, I think—was staring at the boy. She had a very embarrassed expression while he gave her a small smirk, raising the "okay" sign.

I blinked as I kept reading with her, and she didn't particularly seem to mind it.

When we reached the end of the book, she closed it and gazed back at me, smiling slyly. "I knew that would happen."

I smiled and stood when she did, picking up all the tossed manga on the floor and placing them in the shelves within seconds.

I then stopped in front of her, finding her brushing down her sweater. "You like that manga, duchess?"

She gazed up and nodded. "Yes."

"Who is your favorite character?" I wondered then, brushing down her shirt for her.

"The demon," she said then, "duh. He's a badass demon. It's hot."

I then smiled down at her, arching a brow.

She gazed up at me then and narrowed her eyes. "Shut up."

I watched as she moved past me and started to the door. She stopped, gazing down at her attire before looking at me. "Is... everyone in bed?"

I smiled. "Why do you ask?"

"Because I don't want to be seen half-naked walking to my room."

I just stepped past her to the tray of milk. "Yes, they are." I gazed up then as she opened the door and started out. "Did you put that on yourself?"

She just parted her lips before gazing down. "It's comfortable."

"And the bunny ears?" I asked her.

She stared at me for a moment before her cheeks shaded slightly, but she glared. "What about them?"

"I can take them off if you wish. You hated them the moment I put them on you."

She just closed her eyes and tipped her chin up, turning back toward the door. "No, it's fine."

I followed after her when she started to her room, vaguely noticing her pulling the sweater down to hide her underwear. "It looks adorable on you, duchess. It should be a daily attire. People would never suspect you're up to something."

She just grumbled under her breath.

"Do you think I'm lying?" I said as we entered her bedroom.

"I think you're irritating," she retorted.

I just smiled and closed the door behind us, gazing up at her as she sat on her bed.

I set the tray on her nightstand and caught her teacup, holding the milk out to her. "Your nightly beverage, my lady."

She took it then, sipping it immediately.

But I saw her wince a little at the movement, making my lashes lower. "Duchess, did he hurt you?"

She set her cup onto her lap, gazing up at me in boredom. "You asked me that already, I said no."

I just watched her carefully.

But I stepped toward her, leaning down as she sucked in a breath. "Forgive me, my lady," I said quietly, lowering the collar of her sweater.

The moment I saw the wound crusted with dried blood, I sighed and pulled back, gazing down at her. "Must you lie to me, duchess?"

She looked a little embarrassed but attempted to hide it, closed her eyes and sipping her milk again.

I just stepped back and bowed. "I shall be back."

Twenty seconds later, I came back with a bandaging kit, finding Hazel lying on the bed, half-asleep.

I just smiled and closed the bedroom door again, moving over to her and helping her sit up.

She moaned in annoyance as I lifted her sweater over her head and exposed her chest, the only clothing on her was her small, pink underpants.

Before I attended to her wound, though, I helped her into her nightshirt, leaving it unbuttoned so her chest was still exposed.

"If you're tired, you can lay down while I bandage it," I suggested.

She fell backward onto the bed, collapsing as I chuckled.

Finally, I crawled slightly on and caught the kit, pulling out some gauze and hydrogen peroxide, lightly pouring some of the liquid onto the gauze before gazing down at her.

"This might sting, I apologize, duchess."

I then lightly dabbed the wound.

The blood around it sizzled, and Hazel whimpered, tensing.

"I apologize," I said again, finishing cleaning it as her chest heaved up and down uneasily.

Afterward, I just spread on some anti-bacterial ointment and stuck on some bandages, buttoning her shirt seconds later.

Hazel was now staring at me, looking a little flustered for her particular self.

I just leaned down onto the bed, hearing her breath catch ever-so-slightly as my face hovered inches above hers.

"You smell like jasmine and lavender," I said then, watching her eyes and burn with something less innocent.

She just continued staring at me.

But I lowered myself and set my lips on hers.

She gave in for a second, lashes fluttering as she gripped onto my shirt.

But her breath suddenly sucked in, and her body tensed.

I parted my lashes then, worried I broke boundaries.

Her eyes were closed, though... and her hands dropped to her sides.

Did she pass out?

The moment a bitter-sweet taste spread along my tongue, I shoved myself back, covering my mouth with the back of my hand.

Shit...

The taste still lingered in my mouth, pummeling through my senses, but I could ignore it, forcing my heart to slow it's racing.

I gazed down at Hazel then, finding her eyes shut and her breaths quiet. Her movements were stilled, hands set against the bed on each side of her head.

She looked... lifeless.

I just pulled my hand away from my mouth, lashes lowering. "I was afraid this would happen." I gazed down at her more numbly now. "Your wish was granted, duchess, so your blood is now ready for harvest. But I do not want to take it."

I watched her softly, finding her movements gone. "My... you look like a princess in a fairy tale... lost in a deep sleep until true love's kiss wakes her." I leaned down then, brushing her hair away from her face. "There's no need to fear, my lady. I can reenact the contract. I will create new terms for you. I swear on it."

My eyes glowed a dark red as the light in the room vanished, leaving us in darkness.

I felt my pupils slit as another small smile formed onto my lips. "It's time, duchess."

I then leaned down further, tipping her chin up gracefully as she remained asleep.

But I immediately froze, lips inches from hers when my eyes widened.

I pulled back then, staring down at her when frost consumed me. "Wait... where did it go?"

I stared down at her carefully, finding her body lifeless still.

I tipped her chin up further, breaths shaking when I spread my hand along her chest, trying to feel her.

But I immediately drew back, something hot swelling inside me. "No." I sat up then, teeth gritting. "No, it cannot be."

She just remained asleep, but I knew she wasn't dead.

But I couldn't sense it within her. It was gone. But how? It would've come back into her if she was still alive!

The panic settled in then, burning through me like fire.

I just clenched the sheets tightly into my hands, eyes blazing in anger as the shadows in the room deepened.

Someone took it.

They stole what was mine.

My duchess's spirit was taken.

T o be continued in "*A Song of Darkness*"

Don't miss out!

Visit the website below and you can sign up to receive emails whenever Arianna Courson publishes a new book. There's no charge and no obligation.

https://books2read.com/r/B-A-ERCW-HGDGF

BOOKS 2 READ

Connecting independent readers to independent writers.

Did you love *The Wonderland Show*? Then you should read *Vendetta*[1] by Arianna Courson!

He is the reaper of the night.

He is my moving shadow.

He is the darkness swelling inside me.

He is my vengeance.

But he will save me.

Alistair Stormhard was known for his schemes—he was known as the devil hidden in the night—but he will not show unless he deems you worthy.

A worthy meal.

---

1. https://books2read.com/u/bokv6v

2. https://books2read.com/u/bokv6v

It wasn't until he heard my scream that Alistair came, and he promised me one wish. Any wish I desired.

All he wanted in return,

Was my life.

He wanted to drain every ounce of blood from me, for I was a dessert to him. A delicious one.

One he'd been craving for centuries.

Also by Arianna Courson

Chains
Secrets
Bloodless: The Entire Crave Saga

The Fallen Shadow Saga
Lily's Fallen Shadow
Jason's Angel of Storms
Silence Me
Silence Me

The Vendetta Saga
The Demon's Duchess
The Shattered Carnival
City of the Dead
The Wonderland Show
A Song of Darkness
Duchess of Death
Vendetta

Standalone
Obsession
Catch Me if You Can
Catch Me if You Can
Corrupted
The Eleventh Hour

About the Author

Arianna Courson is an author of young adult fiction, specializing in paranormal, fantasy, and romance. She lives in Colorado with her two cats and two dogs and divides her time between writing and enjoying the great outdoors.

Milton Keynes UK
Ingram Content Group UK Ltd.
UKHW030915121124
451094UK00001B/42

9 798227 270634